COME INTO THE LIGHT

STEPHEN O'ROURKE

Mirror Matter Press

Austin, TX

www.mirrormatterpress.com

April 2016

"Come Into The Light" © 2016 Stephen O'Rourke

Cover Art by Matthew Revert

Book Design by Travis Tarpley

CHAPTER 1

Harold went in search of Nora, Bill, and Jordan.
They weren't in their safe place, which might
mean they were probably on the roof. They went
up there to take in the sun sometimes before
going back into their hiding place even though
they were told it was dangerous. Harold has seen
how restless they've been, he has come across
the same restlessness in the past and it usually
led to trouble. Maybe the heat inside their small
apartment, the smell, the darkness, the sense of
claustrophobia and isolation was getting to
them. There was nothing new in that. Harold
has seen it happen before with others he has
tried to help. What he didn't expect was to have
to break through a flimsy barrier and dislodge a
door to get onto the roof. When he saw them
there huddled together looking both defiant and
expectant, staring at him as if they didn't want
him there. He knew they were headed toward
the edge of reason.

Their heat boiled brains couldn't comprehend a single thing that he said as he tried to get them to go with him. They had to get back to their safe place before it was too late. They were making themselves targets with each passing moment. It would be coming soon. Already he could feel the air changing. They must feel it too but they don't seem bothered, anxious or fearful. Their act of defiance was nothing short of crazy.

"We don't want to go back inside." Nora explained in an anguished voice.

"Yea, it's dark and gloomy. We can't breathe." Bill added.

Harold sighed with nervous impatience, "But you're protected."

"We aren't afraid. He won't hurt us. He loves us." Bill said in awed confusion.

"You will be changed. You won't be human anymore. He's playing with your minds."

Harold saw the sun waver strangely as a bright flash of explosive light projected out of it. Morphing and taking shape as it shot toward them across the sky. He felt the stinging, piercing sensation in his head and pushed back against it. It hurt like hell.

"It's here! We have to go!"

They were bent over from the pain in their heads and wouldn't move, even when he shouted in terror and pulled at them. They fought back saying it was alright. He bit his lip in frustration and tried to think of what else to do. This was what they wanted, but he told them they were crazy. Have they forgotten about the others and what happened to them? Despite everything he said they wouldn't listen and if he stayed he would be changed along with them. Made into something cold and alien, a vacant minded worshipper who did what he was told, who did what that thing jetting and forming across the sky wanted him to do. Feeling he had no choice, he turned and fled. Abandoning his friends in order to save himself, he jumped over the clutter in the doorway to escape down the stairs. He didn't feel good about what he was doing but they were stuck stiff in a kind of hypnotic haze. The thing hurtling toward them was already taking residence in their minds and it wasn't about to let go until it had them in its trap. Soon they would be paralyzed and made helpless and he would be trapped just like them and changed into something awful, inhuman if he didn't flee. Once that thing disturbed the air and exploded into your consciousness you had to get as far away from it as you could and dig yourself into a dark hole. If his friends waited much longer it would be too late, yet they had made their choice, he could see it in their faces. Still, a little part of him held onto the hope that they would realize that what they were doing was foolish. That they would see reason before it was too late.

Yet just as Harold was stumbling down eight flights of stairs to make his escape, Nora, Bill, and Jordan were already in the process of raising their heads like attentive followers to the embryo like mass emerging in the light. They soaked up the astounding view unfolding before their eyes in awed amazement even as a deep sense of foreboding bubbled up through their bodies causing a confused adrenalin rush of excitement and terror. They were itching with that intuitive sense to run, to take flight, while still being mesmerized. Yet the warm pressure inside their brains, the incipient itch of needing, of wanting to be overtaken was stealing past their fear.

Getting closer, the embryo like mass inside the light slowed down, weaving and coalescing by degrees into shape. From that shape emerged a face, arms, and legs. A sexless, hairless human shape that opened its fiery golden eyes.

Harold had two more flights to go. He was vaulting down the stairs with a speed that could be easily miscalculated. One bad move and he would be tumbling, smashing his head on the steps... the edges sharp... hard... a possible broken neck. Paralyzed. Helpless. Dead. His heart racing. His legs pounding. So little time... must hurry. It knew of him but was busy now. It wouldn't be for long. So many goddamn steps. What was he thinking; exposing himself like this? No one else took these kind of risks. Another flight, one more, and then the lobby. Ah, there it was, and there was the door to the outside. He leapt over the last clutter of chairs and raced through the lobby; crashing into the door; spraining his wrist as it jammed against the doorknob. He clumsily wrestled with the knob. Trying to turn it again and again, growing anxious. He had to slow down... relax... concentrate. His throat dry and burning as the knob finally popped.

He was out in the street, but nowhere near safe. He looked up toward the roof for only a second to see a black blur in the bright light. Filled with eyes. Eyes that were watching. Don't look.

There was screaming, awful and tortuous, as he turned away from the roof. He couldn't help them. He felt helpless, less than human. Why didn't he do more?

Cars were parked, abandoned. The meters reading violation in red, he continued to run in a trance. A city boiling with hostility. He knew where he should go, but somehow his rubbery legs were taking him in the direction he didn't want to go. He felt alone and scared yet he had to report what happened. He had to let Seth know but not now. It was so very hot. So very goddamn hot and bright. It never changed. The earth had turned into a hot ominous monster, a seething example of overwrought indulgences. The sun never let up and that thing thrived in the light seeming to derive energy from it. He was sweating, God was he sweating. His eyes were already hurting... stinging... watering as he tried to find his way down the street. Might be nice to get some shade, but though the street appeared empty he knew they were out there somewhere ready to grab hold of him, to force him to bend to that thing's will, that monster that they saw as a god. To make him one of them. They probably already knew where he was and now Nora, Bill, and Jordan had joined their ranks. He had to keep going. He didn't know where his sunglasses were and the heat and his head were killing him. He thought he had them in his pants pocket, not that it mattered. They weren't all that helpful. He wore them mostly to give him a sense of comfort, a sense of control that he knew he didn't have.

There was a crash of glass breaking. His eyes darting in all directions. Windows hollowed out of buildings. Shadowy movements within. A rush of bodies. Birds fluttering from ledges. Gray walls stained with graffiti.

The minute he turned on to Second Street he knew he would be going to see his uncle. His uncle was mad. He probably killed himself. Why go there?

Before he gave himself any more time to think about it he was stepping over broken glass and rubble and into the old boarded-up tavern with the apartment above it on Second Street. The place was cleaned out but there were still a few torn up and savaged booths, a scrolled on wall-size mirror, and a dented and gouged walnut bar, minus stools and a metal footrest. The place was dusty, dim, and smelled of piss, shit, and liquor, but Harold couldn't care less. He was heading for the narrow door at the end of the bar, the one next to the coin-operated wall phone that had stopped operating long ago. The door was chipped, worn, and the top hinge had one rusted and one bent screw holding it in place; causing the bottom to scrape along the floor as you pulled on it. There was no light to mark the narrow passage up the tight, moldy steps, so Harold retrieved his trusty butane lighter from his pants pocket. There wasn't much

11

fuel left. The moorings for the banister had long since rotted and the banister had to be torn away and tossed into the trash pile in the basement. The plank steps, too small for his feet, sunk under his weight ready to give at any moment, so he stepped as lightly as he could and tried maintaining his balance at the same time. It was quite a feat, and it left him a little woozy and tired each time. The floor in the short hallway was also soft and unsafe; leaning crookedly. The yellowed wallpaper hung down like sloping tree limbs. The apartment door at the end and to the right had a new combination lock attached to a corrosive eye hook and hasp. With a couple of sweeps of the dial he was in.

When he saw the figure come at him he jumped. It was just the full-length mirror on the wall dimly lit by two gooseneck lamps, but he forgot that it was there directly across from the doorway. There was a thin light flashing ahead of this mirror and suspended in the darkness: a camera was mounted on a small table with a built-in sensor to detect the smallest amount of light and to trigger an alarm. He was surprised it was still working when a low eerie siren sounded causing him to clench with fear until he realized it was the alarm reacting to his lighter so he shut it off. It was creepy seeing his darkened silhouette in the mirror and the flashing red light and nothing else. The boarded-up windows really did an excellent job in keeping out the light and most of the heat, although the tiny apartment was no less suffocating. There was no electricity, no way to get relief except with a battery operated fan which he gave to his uncle. His Uncle Liam was obsessed about his warning system though it made little sense. A warning would give him a few seconds notice before he was dragged out by the 'sunbies' as he called them.

There was a harsh rustling from below the table. The crisp, plastic tablecloth shot up to reveal his uncle staring at him angrily. His milky, owl-shaped eyes were buried beneath heavy lenses and his badly shorn head was peppered with thin bits of lifeless hair. He was one odd specimen and the odor coming off of him was the odor of someone who hasn't bathed in ages. He was still wearing the same old striped shirt and khaki shorts he has always worn, caked in grime, shit, and dust.

"You set off my alarm you turd."

Harold found the button to shut it off and that released a bit of the tension, "Sorry."

He then closed the door and proceeded to feel his way to a chair resting up against a wall to the right of the door. He was too exhausted to stand and grateful to have a chance to rest.

"Something bad happened, didn't it?" Liam asked, smiling strangely.

"I didn't think‑

"I tried to warn you."

"I don't know how you can sound so pleased?"

"Because it's always a mistake to rely on others. Did you think you could come back here and suck off me again?"

"No," Harold shook his head feeling weary, confused, "I don't know."

"You're a wreck."

"I have you to thank for it."

"Don't you dare blame me. You're the one who left."

"And I am glad that I did."

"So why are you here now?"

Harold was about to speak and yet he didn't know what he wanted to say.

"It's not because you miss me, is it? I bet you're surprised that I'm still alive and kicking. I guess you thought I wouldn't survive without you, well get over yourself, boy-o."

Harold was incredulous, open-mouthed with amazement, "Have you been out?"

Uncle Liam stared at him for the longest time as if he had grown a third eye, "Out! No one ever goes out if they know what's good for them!"

"Then, how are you-

"None of your business."

Harold processed all kinds of theories for how Uncle Liam was surviving and none of them sounded good. He was happy to see that his uncle didn't need him. Maybe that was all he needed to know, and maybe he came back here hoping he would find a corpse.

"You're giving me that look. I could always read what was going on in your head. Your mother was the same way."

The mention of his mother sent a shock through him. He would never see either of his parents ever again. The old fuckhead had to mention her, didn't he? He knew how to twist the knife.

"I have to go. I only came here to see how you were doing." He said, standing.

Uncle Liam wasn't angry anymore and he even began to appear friendly, "Why don't you stay around. I was about to have my lunch."

There was a snap and an animal squeaking in pain from somewhere in the back of the apartment. Harold turned in fright. His eyes traveling down the crumbling, bereft hallway in search of the animal, toward the kitchen, the bedrooms, though all he saw was evidence of a shape here or there and the darkness that rose out of it.

"Something bothering you, boy-o."

Harold turned back shrouded in dismay as he stared at his uncle, and then with an anxious kind of sickness stirring in him he grabbed for the door, "I don't know why I came."

Liam laughed sarcastically and wet his lips.

"Be careful closing the door when you leave. It doesn't set right."

As Harold left the bar feeling confused and upset his eyes happened to light on a girl who slipped back into the shadows of a battered laundromat from across the street. She had her eyes on him and she looked curious, guilty as if she has been following him. Harold didn't think she was one of them. He got a feeling for what they were like and this girl didn't give off the empty, worshipful vibe he was accustomed to, yet when he crossed the street to find out who she was and what she wanted she had vanished. He didn't think there were any strays left in the city. How was she able to survive and avoid being changed by that thing? A further sweep of the area continued to leave him puzzled. He has never known anyone who could move so quickly. From what he got of her she was thin with short blond hair and blue, luminous eyes. She was dressed the way a boy would be dressed in an overly large shirt and jeans with sneakers on her feet. There was writing on the shirt: Go Buckeyes. She could have been sixteen or seventeen. A little younger than him. He didn't have the chance to get a good look at her. He wished he knew why she was following him. Seth would want to know about her he realized. He's always looking for strays.

And speaking of Seth, he had to get going. He just remembered there was a meeting taking place this afternoon at 169 Piedmont. The address at Piedmont housed a three story clapboard house painted brown with yellow sashes. The house was once owned by Seth's friend and had been designed with a reinforced shelter in the basement. Seth got possession of it when his friend was found in the basement with a hole in his head from a .32 caliber bullet.

17

CHAPTER 2

Harold had to remember the secret knock before he was let in by Ross who directed him to the living room. As he followed Ross down the long hallway past the foyer he could hear voices upraised and people arguing. They were in the midst of a discussion with Seth who was standing at the front of the room near the boarded up picture window trying to ease concerns as an active group of forty some individuals sat stirring up emotions or rose up from an assembly of plastic chairs to argue. The chairs were in rows and lined out all along the extent of the carpeted room. The plush chairs, tables, lamps, and couches had been pushed aside or shoved up against the nearest walls. Sara saw him come in from the corner of the room and waved to him. He waved back and they traded smiles. She was thin and pretty with long dark hair and it was clear she was interested in him but Harold didn't know what to think of it. They had kissed and she did seem nice but he didn't know if he wanted to take the next step. Sara could sometimes be intolerable, pushing him to do things he didn't want to do.

"We don't even know who we can trust most of the time. They have that weird light in their eyes but most of the time they look and act like us and I bet they have spies."

"We can't let our fears control us. They were just as human as you or I at one time. Let's not forget that they are not to blame for what has happened to them. That thing is to blame not them." Seth argued, keeping his demeanor somber yet forthright.

"I still think they have spies. They're recruiting people all the time. Before you know it we will all be like them if something is not done."

A rousing cheer swept up from all around Jacob. More than half of the room seemed to be on his side. He had this way of speaking that was common yet incendiary. His thinning combed back hair, chisel hard face, and rock solid workman's body gave him the appearance of honest labor, of honest talk. And though he wasn't the type to be agreeable he was born to be a leader. Even the young ones in the crowd seemed drawn to his sense of needing to take action, but Harold didn't like him. He knew that Jacob would never have placed himself at risk to help anyone against that thing. In his mind there was no room for weak individuals. If they gave in they must be destroyed. He thought Harold was foolish and stupid, as foolish and stupid as Seth who gained sympathy and support because of his blindness. Yet Seth was a born leader as well and unlike Jacob he was flush with a crop of wiry gray-black hair expanding outward from his head augmenting the shaded eyes and the friendly round face that sought to charm you at every turn. He stood a head taller than Jacob and his skin, unlike Jacob's, was a burnt bronze.

Seth had seemed to be expecting what Jacob would say so he didn't let the cheers and calls to action bother him. He was even smiling as he lifted up his arms to ask for silence.

"Something will be done but for now we need to concentrate on our food supply, our water. There are people who need our help."

"Everyone knows what needs to be done." Jacob rallied; causing another round of cheering that seemed to gain in intensity.

Rosa had raised her hand to the group and shouted in amidst the cheering, "I want to know where my husband is! He was supposed to be here for this meeting!"

The cheering had slowly ended. It was met by confused stares and recriminations, muted conversations and eyes that darted in Rosa's direction. Harold could see that Rosa was upset and nervous. She was a short, round, motherly type of woman who rarely got nervous. In fact she was normally friendly, outgoing, and always ready to see the good points in anyone. Something was bothering her, something she couldn't comprehend by the way her brows furrowed and her eyes stood straight out. She didn't care what the others were thinking. She wouldn't even look around to hear what they were saying. She was concentrating on just that one thing: her husband, John. John was the silent type, introspective, shy, intelligent and he was much taller than Rosa, unusually thin, scrawny with long arms and legs. He wore these cheap nerdy glasses and told harmless jokes that embarrassed him. He was a neurobiologist before all occupations ceased to have meaning and came up with the theory that certain brains were less susceptible to the sun thing's influence, yet he couldn't explain where the creature came from, what brought it here, or what kind of creature it was yet he told Harold he believed the creature thrived on the sun and its energy, and maybe it thrived on human energy as well.

"I'm sure John was delayed for a good reason, Rosa." Seth said, while turning to her.

Rosa wouldn't speak. She closed her lips in a sullen gesture as if she didn't believe in what Seth was telling her. Seth had relied on Rosa's support and John's during the times when Jacob was attempting to take control. Harold saw a much needed opportunity to end the meeting before the fevered emotions bubbling up in the group got out of hand.

"If I could say something."

"Oh, and who is that, our flighty boy wonder?"

Jacob's comment elicited a sprinkle of laughter and Harold found himself smiling.

"I only need a moment of Seth's time."

"Take all the time you need." Jacob said, followed by more laughter.

Seth followed Harold out to the hallway. He was perfectly at ease and didn't need help walking anywhere inside the house for he knew every corner, every obstacle as if it played an intimate role in his life and he had no trouble swiftly accustoming himself to any changes like the redistribution of furniture in the living room.

"You have bad news. I can hear it in your voice."

Harold told him everything including the hasty decision he made to see his uncle.

"You know he can join us anytime."

"He is too far gone, besides he'd never do it. I've tried, remember?"

Seth nodded, sighing, "And the girl?"

"I'm not sure who she is, but I'll keep an eye out for her. She's vulnerable."

"You're a good lad, Harold."

"I can see why Rosa's worried. John is a man of his word. Maybe I should·

"No, you've done enough today. Plus, you don't sound all that hot."

"My head's killing me."

"What's all the secrecy about?" Sara asked as she came up on them grabbing hold of Harold's arm and putting her head on his shoulder while smiling up at him.

"Have you found another girl?"

Before Harold could answer her Seth brought out an assembly of pain killers from his pocket giving Harold a choice, then he insisted that Harold lay down upstairs and rest. Harold was grateful for the order. Sara could sometimes overwhelm him, leave him speechless, now at least he had an excuse for telling her that his head hurt and he needed to rest. He'd see her later.

"Maybe I'll see you sooner than that."

Sara released his arm and bopped his nose with her finger, giving him a mischievous grin before turning and slipping back into the living room.

Harold laughed when he crashed onto the bed. He wondered what she meant.

☼ ☼ ☼

The kiss placed on his lips sometime later woke him. Sara was standing over his bed biting back the need to smile as her eyes dared him to speak. When Harold saw how close she was to him he was immediately aware that he was naked under the sheets, sitting up in his bed with a stunned look on his face. His clothes scattered on the floor probably next to her feet.

"You wanted someone to wake you, didn't you?"

"Oh yea, of course." He said. His words rushed. Her closeness leaving him helpless.

Sara stood up slowly and eyed him with curiosity, "Well, I'm that someone."

"I don't know what to say."

She smirked and gave him a questionable look, "You know your breath smells, boobala."

He's not sure where she got the nickname but she thought it fit him. He didn't mind it all that much but he did mind her being there.

"Sorry. I'll remember to freshen my breath next time you decide to surprise me."

"Do I detect irritation?"

"It's not that I mind, it's just that-

She sighed, "You're a secret person. You like your privacy."

"Something like that." He confessed, yet when he saw she was taking it wrong he told her that he did like the kiss.

"I hope so, because I wonder sometimes if you like me at all."

"I do." He said, blushing, though the words faltered in his mouth.

Sara crossed her arms and directed her eyes away from him, "Okay, okay, I'll give you your privacy if you want it so badly."

"Oh, come on, don't be mad."

"I'll be whatever I want to be."

She stormed out closing the door hard behind her but Harold couldn't say that it bothered him. In fact he was glad that she gave him the opportunity to dress. He would have to talk to her, smooth things over. She was in a different place than him in the relationship. He thought he made it clear he liked to take things slowly, but he wondered if there was something more to it. Girls continued to frighten him in that way. He has never gone all the way with any girl. He wasn't even sure of his emotions. Maybe there was something wrong with him. He should know what he feels. It was all so confusing. He was afraid he was only going to hurt Sara or she hurt him. He liked her as a friend and he didn't want to lose the friendship. Oh what the hell, why can't it be simple.

John was back and Rosa was all over him with worry and relief. She had hugged him so hard he was out of breath. He apologized saying they broke off into two groups and lost track of each other. He had Amanda, Circe, and Adam with him and they were tired. Adam was Seth's teenaged son and Amanda and Circe were tough women with short haircuts who served in the military for nearly twenty years. They were part of John's scouting team. There were a number of scouting teams and everyone took turns doing reconnaissance and scouting for supplies.

"I'm afraid there isn't much left we could find." John said, looking shy and somewhat guilty. Rosa held his face in her hands and gave him a hard kiss on the lips.

The four slipped off their backpacks and laid them on the dining room table for everyone to scrounge through.

"The lab didn't have any chemical inhibitors for the brain but there were some pain killers, antiseptic medicines, bandages, gauzes, tranquilizers at the hospital, although this is the last of them. I don't think we're going to find anymore unless there's a gas station in operation somewhere and we can steal a set of wheels."

"You know what happened the last time we tried to get out of the city, John."

John nodded. He was all too aware of what happened but they had few choices left, "If only I had those inhibitors, Seth. I believe that thing couldn't get inside our heads and control us then, or at least not to the extent of preventing us from leaving."

"We'll get them somehow."

"What's this? Is this the best you could do?" Jacob asked, holding up cans of kidney and wax beans and directing most of his anger at John even as his team defended him.

"All the food shelves are empty. We had to dig those out. They were stuck underneath the shelves. Must have rolled under-

"Just watch what my team can do. This is pitiful." Jacob threw the cans down making a crash on the table like he was using his fists.

"Well, I'm sorry Jacob but-

"Never mind. You did what you could."

Jacob made it clear that he meant it as an insult as he distributed the cans and the group dispersed saying their goodbyes before going out the door heading to their individual shelters.

When they were outside and away from busy eyes, Amanda and Circe had pulled in close

to Jacob to give him their report. They told him they were able to hook up with the supplier. He and his group had an impressive arsenal of weapons and the supplier was willing to work with them. Jacob asked if John and Adam were suspicious of the delay. Amanda said that John had accepted their explanation but she wasn't sure Adam did. Circe confirmed Amanda's assessment.

"I could give a rat's ass about that brat. Did you store the weapons where I told you to?"

They confirmed that they did.

"When do we move?"

"I'm still fleshing out a few people, but I think it will be soon. The time for indecision is done."

CHAPTER 3

Amy saw herself as some kind of jungle cat, capable of slipping in and out of doorways and alleyways without being noticed. She was sly and light-footed. One of her many talents. A nimble tigress out for a jaunt. Zoning in on the sheep people whenever they came in range and dropping back before they noticed her. Sometimes their eyes held the golden shine of their leader, their god as they realized they were being watched and shifted their gaze toward her. Most of the time they were no different from everyone else, the others who were not sheep, or not the same kind of sheep. Amy has lived long enough to know that none of it mattered. She would always be an outsider and more so once the unchanged joined the ranks of the changed and became worshippers under one god. A prospect that was inevitable given the evidence she has seen and stored in her mind. She was not only a cat but a scientist as well, a detective. And though she took on this role she didn't care anything about the outcome devised for these people. They had forsaken her long ago. If she had to be truthful she would prefer to be alone, not changed or unchanged. The only one of her species. The design of things, of DNA. No one liked the way she thought, the way she didn't like to be touched, and her sensitivity to noises, how she hated crowds and became nervous around people never knowing what to say, feeling like an actor playing a part in order to please the people around her, in order to be liked, accepted. Forget that. Why must she give so much and them so little? So she was weird, so what, it was who she was. A doctor from long ago said her brain wasn't normal. He defined her as autistic. A freak of nature and science, of social development. Improved mental acuity only made her more of a social leper. What counted most were social skills, without them you might as well be a ghost.

She had run across that boy again coming out of the abandoned bar: Ned's. He disturbed her, made her feel things she didn't want to feel, made her think things she would rather forget because she had no chance with him. What did she want from him anyway? He was normal. If he touched her she would feel alarmed, feel like she was suffocating. And the idea of kissing. She didn't know why it was done. Who would anyone want to do that? None of it made sense to her. So why was she bothered? Why have these feelings if she didn't want to act on them? Why should she let some boy torment her? She knew her place. She knew where she was happiest. She was no fool. So she should let it drop. Put him out of her mind. Yet every time she said she would do just that she got the itch to look at him, to pretend at something that wasn't real, would never be real. Well, as long as it was pretend she would be alright. Watching him from afar, then capturing all those images of intimacy between them in her mind to masturbate to afterwards. It was all she needed to make herself happy. She has no reason to feel guilty, strange. She has a right to pleasure too. And by this means she would never have to feel awkward and inadequate in front of him. He would never have to descend into someone mean or cruel, someone who would laugh at her or be disgusted by her, someone far removed from the image she had placed on him. He could remain high in her mind as someone who might care for her no matter what she was like.

She wondered what sort of relationship the boy had with the madman living up above the bar. She has snuck in to listen to him rant numerous times. It became one of the highlights of her day. She enjoyed his ranting. It tickled her. She liked it that he was crazier than her. He seemed to be pleading at one point and threatening at another. Cackling as he claimed he had outwitted the sun god, that the dark would protect him. She heard him eat, heard him wrestle with his food, heard the many tortuous pleas from the living vermin before they were silenced.

Amy wondered if the boy, and she called him boy even though he was older than her, knew he was in danger. That some of the people in his group were working behind the scenes to make a lot of bad things happen. She wondered if she should warn him. No, she had to keep her distance, keep moving. He would find out eventually and so would the sheep. She certainly wouldn't warn them not after what they tried to do to her.

The sheep tried to change her that one time but she couldn't be changed. Their sun god couldn't get inside her mind. They had held her, forced her to stare into the light as it came for her, yet her mind proved too large a task for their sun god. She felt the probing, the forceful acts of entry that suddenly became erratic, confused, then disappeared altogether forming the oscillating echoes of bewilderment, of facing up against something that was unknown to it. They had let her go, shaking their heads in disapproval as she left them. These days they do everything they can to avoid her, not that they could ever catch her again now that she has become a jungle cat, a covert operative sweeping over the landscape of the city in search of entertainment and information.

And speaking of entertainment wasn't that the sunbies removing graffiti, hammering boards and replacing windows. Industrially attempting to remake the past, to get the city back in order. She must say it showed a remarkable amount of ambition, and also showed just how cruelly warped their sun god was. If only they knew what she knew. She felt guilty about laughing at them but she couldn't help herself.

CHAPTER 4

Harold saw Jordan's clothes scattered about outside the apartment building and his ring lying next to the curb. There were thin white fragments bathed in a puddle of blood on the sidewalk that looked like grounded bones. He shivered to think that that is what they were: human bones. In his mind he saw Jordan jumping from the roof, but if his clothes, his ring, were here where was he? Harold has seen plenty of people commit suicide in order to avoid the fate of the sunbies. He could have had a late change of mind, but that still didn't answer the question. Where was Jordan? Come to think of it where were all the others who took their lives? How could they all have vanished? This wouldn't have happened if he hadn't run away.

He was sitting on the steps outside the apartment building holding the bone fragments in his hand with a care that was near heartrending when he looked up to see Nora and Bill standing at the bottom of the steps. He nearly swallowed his tongue when he saw them. They observed his reaction without emotion, though something golden slithered to life in their eyes.

"We knew we'd find you here." Nora said in a voice that was both pleasant and remote.

Harold's mind was racing. He couldn't speak.

"We appreciate that you were worried but there is no need for worry. We are among good folk and we couldn't be happier. Our lord has provided us with electricity and real food and water. You don't know how good it is for us. We're rebuilding, starting a new life."

"You should see it the way we see it. He truly means the best for us. No more headaches, no more fear, no more hunger. He has brought us to the light." Bill added, bending his lips into a blissful smile that Nora sees and imitates before turning back to Harold.

"You don't know how good your life can be. All you have to do is reach out to the light. The light will free you; the light will make you whole."

Harold wanted to laugh and to cry. The two people standing before him weren't Nora and

Bill anymore, that sun thing had gotten inside them and had taken over their minds just like he knew it would. He was the golden flash in their eyes the smile that functioned to disarm you. Harold liked to believe that maybe Nora and Bill were still in those bodies somewhere fighting for their existence. He had to believe that. He couldn't live with himself if he didn't.

"You're wasting your time with me."

"We are all worthy of his love."

He felt sick. He didn't want to hear another word.

"Please go away."

"What do you have there?" One of them asked in a voice that sounded accusatory.

Harold saw them staring at his hand. They almost appeared to be sneering at what they saw there so he put the fragments in his shirt pocket, "Just things I like to collect."

He was getting anxious. They were making him anxious.

"Listen, if you don't mind there's somewhere I need to be. So if you would·

The smiles were gone from their faces. He could sense hostility, a type of determination. Their eyes burned with that golden light once again but this time there was a sharpness in those eyes, an intensity that was menacing, and when he got up to leave they blocked his path.

"What are you doing?" He asked, trying to smile.

They avoided the question, zeroing in on him with the alertness of attack dogs, ready to strike if he made a move.

He nervously looked about. There wasn't anyone who could help him and he didn't have a weapon, something Jacob said they should have at all times. He wasn't sure he would be able to use a weapon even if he had one but still it would have been nice knowing he had it on him. He would have to go around them, outsmart them somehow, but before he could make a move there was a ring of gunfire. Blood shot out from Nora's neck and Bill's chest and he was splattered by their blood before they collapsed on top of him. He screamed in shock as he fell back with them on top of him. Their bodies were riddled with bullets and they were groaning in pain. Suffocating under the weight of blood pouring into their lungs. With sudden terror he pushed the riddled bodies out of his way and tried to free himself even as they floundered in a panic and snatched at him. Then someone got hold of his flaying hands and worked to pull him free with a few quick jerks. He looked up to see it was Ross, the bodybuilder and sometime guard. Ross asked him if he was alright and he mumbled that he was. Still trying to understand what had happened. Ross got him to his feet just as Harold saw Jacob plant a bullet into Bill's skull then Nora's.

When the back of their skulls came loose with the impact Harold leaned over to vomit. He wiped his mouth and shivered. Ken, Jacob's friend and ally with lighter, thicker hair and freckles, was standing beside Jacob smiling. In fact all three of them were smiling above the bloodied mess lying still at their feet. It was macabre. And when they turned to look at him, almost in unison, he felt a chill.

"You should be glad we followed you here. You ought to know better than to go out on your own, boy wonder. You've been told how dangerous it is?"

Harold didn't like the lecture. Who was he to tell him what to do and what not to do?

"What are you doing with weapons? You're not supposed to-

"What…. save your life?" Ken asked him.

"This punk, I don't know. He doesn't even know what's good for him." He added as an aside to Jacob.

Harold knew he should be grateful but anything he said would sound false. He hadn't gotten over the shock of those bullets to the brain.

There was a change in the air around them. Jacob, Ken, and Ross noticed it too and winced, becoming alarmed. Harold could feel the pressure in his head, the familiar intrusion.

"Come on, we have to go before it gets here!"

"What do we do with the bodies?"

"We haven't the time! Leave them!"

Jacob instructed Harold to follow and he did blindly. They turned the corner of the street just as the sun wavered and a golden light shot out of it transforming into a large golden spider as it approached and swooped down on Nora and Bill. The spider clipped its mandibles and began tearing into the bodies devouring everything in order to absorb the pools of energy that still remained in the cooling bodies. When the spider had finished and leapt out of sight all that was left of Nora and Bill was their jewelry, clothes, and a few scattered bones. In time, these items would be lifted up by the wind and blown in all directions.

When the four had gotten as far away as their breath would take them they stopped and looked back. They no longer had the feeling that they were in danger though they kept walking. Harold knew by the way he was slowly surrounded by the three men that he wouldn't be going back to his Piedmont address. Jacob explained that he couldn't trust him not to snitch and he wasn't about to try anything with them armed.

"I know you don't like me but I like you. You're a good kid. Just a little screwed up is all. I like to believe in happy endings but eventually you have to face the facts. You have to take charge."

Harold was brought to Amanda's house on Colder Avenue where he was escorted to an upstairs room. The room smelled stale but not offensive and had a laminated wooden floor, plain blue wallpaper, and was bare. As clean of dust as the rest of the house.

Amanda asked him if he wanted his shirt cleaned making him aware that he still had Nora and Bill's blood on him. With a frenzy of nervousness he took off his shirt and gave it to her.

A wet washcloth was provided for his face and neck. His pants and shoes had tiny pinpoints of blood and he ended up removing them as well leaving him in his underwear. His face flushed as he handed over the items but Amanda took no notice of his embarrassment.

He wiped the blood off his face and neck with extreme care. The cold water was refreshing, stimulating, but he was happy to hand the soaked red cloth back to Amanda. Ross went and got him a towel to dry his face. When he was finished he handed the towel back to Ross and the door to the room was closed and locked. They wouldn't answer his questions.

When he thought they were well away from the door he tried to jimmy the lock with his fingers before backing against the door to think. He listened to the conversation milling up to his ears from the ground floor but understood little of it. Jacob was doing most of the talking. And as the conversation ceased and he heard a door closing he suddenly felt alone. What was he going to do? The windows were blocked and there was no other way out. They left him with an illuminating glow stick that gave off a subtle blue light and not much else.

Out of sheer frustration and exhaustion he slid to the floor, sitting and waiting for what he did not know.

How long were they going to keep him there? Someone at Piedmont was bound to notice him missing. Seth, Adam, John, Rosa, even Sara would wonder where he was, or maybe they have been made prisoners too. Was this Jacob's plan all along? Adam had his suspicions but Seth closed his ears to them. It was known that Adam didn't trust Jacob, and why did any of that matter now. The fact is he was a prisoner and he had no idea of what was going to happen to him. He should have told Jacob that he wouldn't say anything, but even he believed that was a lie. Jacob was no fool.

It was dark, even with his eyes adjusting to it, the room was much too dark. He thought by now he would have gotten used to darkness. It was expected given the situation they all were put in but it's never an easy thing to overcome.

The whole house was quiet and the silence had a presence all its own. He could hear every creak, every groan the house was making as if shifted in its frame. Eventually all those groans and creaks became a type of lullaby soothing him into sleep and even as his eyelids began to droop he thought he might as well rest, what else could he do? He was their prisoner for now and he might as well make the best of it.

CHAPTER 5

He felt the glare. There was light burning against his eyelids. That was impossible. He was in a darkened room. Where could the light be coming from? He opened his eyes and there he saw it, there was light pouring out between the cracks in the boarded up windows. Light seeping through every pore as it flowed like liquid golden syrup down off the windows and into the room. The golden syrup formed pools that narrowed into rivers, slithering in serpentine fashion across the floor toward him. He followed its progress with curiosity and then with alarm. The liquid light was climbing up his feet, through his toes, and onto his legs, his mid-section, thickening over him with unbelievable speed, covering him in a golden cocoon. He could feel a hundred tiny touches on his skin, a thousand, like there were legions of centipedes tracing a pathway up through his body. The light was all the way up to his chest by this point, yet when he tried to move, to push himself up, he couldn't.

He felt weighed down, stung, numb. He opened his mouth to shout but he couldn't make a sound. The tiny touches were becoming more aggravated, more insistent as the light reached his neck and encircled it, strangling him. He opened his mouth for air as tiny golden spiders broke free from the cocoon of light and swam into his mouth, filling up his throat, his lungs until his air passages were cluttered with their tiny wiggling bodies then blocked altogether. He strained to breathe, strained to cough out the golden terrors but he couldn't. They were planting eggs inside him, distributing them along the lining of his stomach. Soon they will breed and devour him. He was suffocating. It was the worse feeling imaginable. His heart beat fast with the loss of oxygen and he felt himself slipping, passing out. He was going to die and yet the golden light kept pouring in, engulfing him in its immensity. Seeping up his nose then blinding him. Wrapping itself across every inch of his skull until his head felt like it was going to crack open. There was this beating sound, beating, beating, and then-

He jerked awake. He was in the room. The room that had become his prison and nothing had changed. There was no light, no tiny bugs crawling along his skin, just him curled up on his side against the door with the blue glow stick now barely registering a glow near his open hand. He sat up feeling woozy, unable to figure out what happened. Was he dreaming? Yet it didn't feel like a dream. It felt too real to be a dream, more like a vision of some kind. And then as he thought of this he became all too aware of the pain in his head. It was powerful and bad as if someone had rammed a rod through his skull and twisted it. He didn't know he was screaming until he heard Amanda's voice on the other side of the door asking him if he was alright.

"My head is killing me! God, it hurts so bad!"

"This better not be a trick."

When Amanda unlocked the door moments later she had to ask him to move, yet even the little bit it took for him to roll away from the door put him in agony.

He was crouched in a fetal position holding his head and praying for the pain to go away when Amanda and Circe came to him. Circe held him roughly in her arms and straightened him up against a wall so that Amanda could feed him the pills and the cup of water to swallow them down with. He was sweating, dripping with moisture.

"You don't look at all well."

She was holding the glow stick in her hand when he opened up his eyes to look at her. She had twisted the stick back into life so there was proper illumination once again. She was holding the stick in her hand and the blue glow that bathed her face gave her the appearance of a ghost.

"Those pills will do the trick. They're not the useless crap Primrose has been supplying us with."

When Harold heard her speak of John in that unflattering tone he had the notion to ring her neck even as the pain in his head, though subsiding, was still formidable.

"Just look at him. He's like a weak little puppy." Circe said, from somewhere above him. She seemed to be enjoying his pain.

"What else can you expect? Jake is a fool for thinking he is worth the bother."

"What is in those pills?" Harold asked.

"You sound amazed. I bet you didn't know you could feel so good."

Harold had to admit. The pain was going away pretty quickly and the relief that followed in its footsteps was nearly orgasmic.

"I do believe our boy wonder is one glad puppy. Now you know how it feels to be on the right side of things. Let us know if you need anything else."

Harold closed his eyes and smiled, riding the wave of relief as Amanda and Circe left him alone. One half of him heard the door close and lock while the other half of him still wondered what was in those pills.

CHAPTER 6

Quite a few unchanged humans still managed to be curious about the god who came out of the sun despite what they had heard, and different numbers of these curious folk came each day to the sunbies stronghold at the northern end of the city to witness this god. It was said that this god was the one and true god of all the people, the god of legend, the maker and destroyer of all things, and that he had left his heavenly abode to be with his people in their time of need so that he could salvage souls for the coming apocalypse.

Many now were standing in a long line with stark, curious, oddly wondrous faces. They had ended their pilgrimage and were now at the rudiment of his glory: the public square. His presence could be uniquely felt and seen there. It's where the sunbies gathered to worship. And as the pilgrims flooded in they were welcomed by an excited throng of sunbies who smiled and spoke of the admiration they felt for the pilgrims. Their forbearance and faith was held as a shining example of good will in a time of ugliness. The pilgrims smiled in embarrassment, a bit overwhelmed by the attention given to them, saying that everyone needs faith especially now, and that the true spirit that resides in all people will eventually be recognized.

The sunbies nodded in delirious agreement and couldn't wait to show the pilgrims just what they had achieved under his guidance and leadership. The progress they've made in rebuilding. The home schooling. Their stockpile of supplies and food. Their random forms of electrical power. All of which astounded the pilgrims. The sunbies were living in luxury compared to what they had been facing. So much of what they had been told was wrong.

Amy watched from afar as these pilgrims were being guided about. Though her nature was to mock them she couldn't do it. Instead she felt sad and lost; worried that she didn't have their faith and never would. They wanted so much to believe that their fond wishes had finally been realized that the goodness of God's love would protect and nurture them against the horrors that they face. Yet they had no idea of what they have walked into, of what they would be giving up. They sat in assembly with the sunbies in the public square to watch the sun god appear and take human shape, reciting his vow in a powerful, mesmerizing voice to be a good caretaker of his people before stepping off the stage and milling among his people, projecting a charming smile as he welcomed the pilgrims into the fold and touched hands and faces, bathing those hands and faces in the warm golden light that was pouring out of him.

The pilgrims were so impressed by his golden presence that you could see some of them crying and some singing, raising their hands up to him to be blessed. They had no idea that they would never be allowed to leave, and even as some were happy to stay, a few were forced to bow to his presence and be rendered hollowed out puppets to his parasitic intrusion. And if they prove useful they could be chosen for the right to ascend.

Amy has seen this feeding ritual clothed as an ascension done many times and it never got any less creepy. The ascension begins with the chosen ones being laid out on constructed wooden stages in the public square where they are injected with a serum that puts them into a deep hallucinogenic sleep. There they await their ascension as the other sunbies stand in a circle and watch as well as pray. When the sun god appears he opens his arms out to the chosen ones with a bright flourish producing an intense ball of blinding light that engulfs the sleepers and once the light has been lifted the sleepers are then supposedly lifted up into that light, but Amy knows this is not what happens, she knows of the monstrous golden spider that leaps down on the sleepers and devours them because the light is not always blinding, not that the sunbies would notice. The sunbies hear, see, and believe only what the creature allows them to hear, see, and believe. In their minds, the chosen have been given an early ticket to heaven. A blessing brought about by their unwavering obedience. Even when the chosen realize they are not hallucinating and call out in anguish, their cries are heard as praise, as expressions of ecstasy, giving the sunbies reason to rise up and cheer.

Until most recently the pilgrimages, the rebuilding, and the ascension rituals have become common practices but lately there have been disruptions, disruptions that have left the sunbies in a foul and angry mood. Terrorists have upset their very existence, their religious faith and a war has begun as Amy had anticipated and this war has lowered her options, forcing her out of her role as spectator where she must hide in the midst of gunfire and explosions. And when the time is right the jungle cat will reemerge again.

CHAPTER 7

He swallowed a few more doses and dropped his head back to wait for the relief that would wash over him. He was asking for the pills more than he was asking for food or water now but he didn't care. The relief he felt was unexplainable. His head was abuzz and dreamy and anytime he felt threatened by headaches or by nightmare visions the little oval pills would come to his rescue.

They had found new clothes for him to wear and he was let out to wash in an upstairs bathroom sink or to relieve himself. Amanda and Circe couldn't stand it when he stank. He was visited by Jacob and a few of his supporters on occasion. Sometimes they would gather inside his tiny room and tell him of their efforts why he sat there glassy-eyed. Tell him what results their campaign was having. How surprised the sunbies were. How they were taking over their northern stronghold piece by piece. How the city would one day be free of their kind. That they were not afraid.

No mention was made of the creature. How they expected to defeat it. And no mention was made of setbacks, of troubles that had come up, even though Harold could see the nervous looks he got, the attempts to smile and pretend everything was fine while their minds plagued them with thoughts.

He asked for the umpteenth time what had happened to his friends and the response he got was the same, no one would tell him anything. Then one day he heard the lock click on the door and the door swung open to reveal Sara standing before him. Her hair was shortened and she was thinner. She was otherwise in a ragged state looking as though she hadn't slept as she eyed Harold with sadness then with anger.

"Look at you. You're pathetic."

It was true he had puked and hadn't yet washed that day but was she being fair?

"Sara."

"Yea, it's me."

"You're alright."

He had been so worried. He spent every hour and minute wondering if she had been imprisoned like him or murdered.

"They kept me here. Jacob he-

She put up her hands to quiet him and suddenly she looked even more tired, "I know all about it."

He smiled, "I'm glad you're okay."

"Yea, well, I'm not that okay, alright."

Her voice was listless, strained. In the past she had been argumentative toward him or teasing; now she just seemed far away.

Harold made an attempt to stand but he was weak so Sara had to help him. Sara went to get him a washcloth so he could wipe off the puke and when he tried to apologize she wasn't listening. He was shaking just in the effort to stand. It was what the pills had done to him. For the first time in he didn't know when he felt ashamed, not only for being a drugged out zombie but for ignoring his conscience.

"Things are bad, Boobala. You should know that."

He had heard the gunfire, the explosions, some from faraway and some from up-close but

the good thing about the pills was he didn't have to care. None of it seemed related to him. If the floor beneath him exploded he would probably laugh and find it all so funny. Lose a limb here or there, it was all one great big farce.

"He's crazy, you know."

Sara's eyes cut into Harold, "All of us have found the need for compromise. You shouldn't place the blame entirely on him."

Harold widened his smile by a few degrees, fighting off the need to sit down and make himself comfortable. He directed his eyes at Sara and kept himself focused no matter how difficult a task it proved to be.

"The last time I saw you you were angry with me. I guess some things don't change."

Her gaze was even more intense than his pretended to be yet there was a tenderness that hadn't been there before. Her hand reached up to play with his greasy, sweaty hair, and this half attempt at playfulness drew a spark of that old fondness in her face. When he reached up to take her hand in his however she froze at his touch and freed her hand. When he stepped forward for a kiss she backed away.

"No, don't."

She wouldn't look at him. Her eyes were jetting about as if she felt trapped, ready to flee.

"I only came to see you because Jacob wanted me to."

Her eyes caught his once more in defiance, "I'm in firm agreement with what he's doing. I'm fighting alongside some very courageous people. You wouldn't understand. "

His smile faded and his legs were shaking once again. He felt the ache of loneliness rise in him, "I guess I wouldn't."

"I don't want to hear it, Boobala. I don't want you whining. I thought you were dead or had been turned over into one of those sunbies, and you might as well know that Adam and I have become a couple. He's not like you; he has real passion for me. He was even willing to betray his father for me."

Harold didn't know what to say. The words were caught in his throat. Yet he wanted to reach out and hug Sara more than anything. There was just something so pitiful, so loathsome in her voice that all he could do was hold her in his arms. Surprisingly she didn't pull away when he embraced her and when she started to cry he began to cry too.

When she was about to leave she told him that he would have to stay off the pills if he wanted any further information from her. He could see the scars on her hands, her face, how dirty she had become. And to his horror he had noticed that she was missing a finger.

"I'm really happy for you, Sara; I just want you to know that."

"Yea, well, so what if you are."

☼ ☼ ☼

As it turned out he didn't have to keep his promise to Sara because his supply of pills had dried up and there was no one around to resupply him. When he came out of the fog he realized that he hadn't had any visitors for some time and that Amanda and Circe were no longer crating him back and forth to the bathroom and taking care of him.

He was starting to worry. There were no sounds in the house, no noises that would indicate there was anyone in the house. What was he going to do? He hadn't realized how important Amanda and Circe had become to him. They were his lifeblood. Yet there was no reason to panic. He would be alright for a while. They will show up, they always do. He just had to be patient.

He tried to pretend that he would be alright but each moment was making him anxious. He waited and waited and still he couldn't hear a single soul coming to his rescue anywhere, even the explosions and gunfire had subsided. He was engulfed by absolute silence and it went on and on until he thought he would go mad. He screamed out Amanda and Circe's names but there was no reply. He called out to anyone to help him but his only companion was the silence. He had begun to sweat and shiver, to twist and turn in agony, overcome with pain and nausea.

He rolled back and forth in that little room singing and humming to himself, trying to lock out the worse of it, wishing he could die rather than feel the way he felt. His voice turned raw from screaming and eventually after he vomited a few times he passed out.

CHAPTER 8

The explosions shook the house waking him. There was rapid gunfire coming in close, some explosions further away. It felt like the house was being rooted off its foundation. The boards on the windows shook and cracked. The floor was rocking beneath him. He didn't understand what was going on. Dust was falling from the ceiling and the ceiling had begun to buckle. He was going to be crushed as explosions and gunfire continued to rain down on him. Overcome by a nervous frenzy he rolled to one corner of the room and stayed there trying to figure out just what was happening.

There were a number of close impacts and each impact loosened boards from the windows letting in the sunlight. One window was cracked and the ceiling continued to bulk and though he knew he must act he just sat there frozen until he heard something smash against the door. There was another smash and another until the door gave way. Harold watched in confusion as these people poured into the room. He saw a face here and there as they turned in his direction. They looked like nightmare images in the mottled mix of shadow and light. So they had come back for him after all, they hadn't forgotten. He tried to speak to express his sense of betrayal and anger but the words that came out made little sense as Jacob lifted him off the floor and spoke rapidly into his ear, telling him they had to go. Ross took the other arm helping to hold him up as they half carried half walked him out the door. He had little strength in his legs but each step worked to restore some mobility. Four men were ahead of them with satchels hanging from their belt loops carrying rifles. They acted as point men, guards.

The house was truly rocking now. They were being bombarded by slabs of plaster and dust that rained down on them from all sides. The stairs were wobbly and uncertain but they managed to get to the ground floor just as a loud explosion blew out a wall and a boarded up window nearby.

They proceeded out of the house and into the midst of chaos. Colder Avenue had been turned into a war zone. You didn't know who was on what side in the battle. It was nothing less than a confusing mess with dead and injured bodies everywhere and people shouting out orders, people screaming in agony.

A man in the forefront of their group was shot in the chest before he returned fire and collapsed. Harold remembered that this was Scott, the carpenter. He had become the movement's handy man and sometime plumber. Ken checked for a pulse while keeping his rifle positioned to fire. He got up and shook his head and they started out again. Shortly after that a grenade was lobbed a few yards from them and there was an explosion. Harold was on the ground bleeding. There was smoke, tear gas, he couldn't see where anyone was or whether they were hurt. Someone had grabbed hold of his legs and was pulling him off the street and into an alley, inside a door. The door slammed and it was pitch black, dark. There was more gunfire and screaming from outside and he was breathing badly, scared. He heard a voice near his ear telling him to breathe slowly, to calm down. It didn't sound like Jacob but the voice was so low, whispery that it could have been anyone. He tried getting up but was pulled down. He was told it wasn't safe.

He heard someone outside call out his name. He got up to respond and felt the blow to his head that left him unconscious.

Sometime later he opened his eyes, blinking in astonishment at the shelves of books and the candlelight. With the effort it took to think he realized he was in the basement of the central library where the reference section was. How did he get here and why? His head hurt like mad, he knew that much, even sitting up had caused a wave of pain and dizziness but he had to know what was going on. He touched his hand to the spot where he received the blow and felt a gauze pad surrounded by band aids over the spot. The area around the pad was sticky with dried blood and he saw that someone had patched his arm. He had a nose bleed but it wasn't anything serious and his eyes felt dry, swollen. He reached in his pocket for the pain killers that were no longer there and when he realized what he had done he had to laugh. The laugh came out hollow, echoing within the labyrinth of the library. He didn't care who heard him. There were those remnants of his withdrawal still clinging to him: the shakiness, the tremors, the nausea, and yet everything felt remote next to the pain.

He can hear his name being called out. Who was it that called out to him? He never had the chance to find out. Did anyone survive the blast? He had to make sense of this.

Eventually his need to find answers and to find whoever had cold cocked him had led him across the reference section to the double wooden doors. The dizziness and pain he experienced made him dependent on the rows of book shelves to keep him upright but the important thing was he was able to stand, to move, and if he kept working his legs his muscle strength would come back. With one long breath he exhaled and tried turning the knobs on the doors but they wouldn't turn. Of course why should they? At the paramount of his frustration he shouted to be let free but no one responded. He shouted a few more times than gave up.

He spent the next few hours, or at least it seemed like hours, carrying a candlestick in one hand as he walked back and forth through the aisles of books to get his legs in condition. It tired him out to the point where the ache in his legs almost matched the ache in his head yet he thought he might as well use his time productively if he was going to stay here a while.

What was it about him that made him the perfect candidate to be someone's prisoner, someone's punching bag? He was beginning to get the notion that he was nothing more than a test dummy being tossed about in a crash, yet it wasn't right and damn it he was going to remedy the situation.

He thought about what he would do as he walked repeatedly up and back and each step took him closer to a feeling of anger. He tried controlling the anger but couldn't. He pulled at the heavy books on the shelves until they came free and then he tossed them on the floor or threw them at the shelves or at the walls, knocking over a candlestick with one of the historical novels and nearly causing a fire. He tried everything he could to dampen his anger but nothing worked. He tried closing his eyes, clenching his teeth, yet all that brought up was the time his mother refused to let him in the room with his grandmother because she was sick and might die. He was eight at the time and he didn't care he wanted to see his grandma, see how sick she really was.

Grandma was coughing and she looked very weak, drawn. She coughed a lot but she waved Harold over to tell him of her dream. She saw horrible things, people with golden eyes and mad grins encircling her, people bloody and dying on the streets, and in the sky something hovered, something watched. She could feel its eyes on her, hear its laughter. All of what his grandmother was telling him sounded strange and yet she went on in a kind of feverish need to explain that it didn't feel like a dream that it felt too real, too immediate like she was being warned. She held onto Harold's hands, grasping them tightly in hers even as she trembled. She fixed her gaze on him in a kind of desperate plea and wouldn't let go, telling him that she was frightened for him, for his future, for all their futures. Harold tried pulling away from her grasp, tried telling her that everything will be fine even as the planet was heating, there was outright warfare, and people were hungry. His schoolmates said that God would help them. He was crying by the time his grandmother let go of her grasp and Harold's mother flew in and pushed him out of the room saying he would be punished. There was no greater punishment than seeing his grandmother groan and take on so after that until one day soon her heart would stop and he would attend her funeral. He never got to talk to his grandmother again. His parents said she had lost her mind. That they didn't want Harold to see her this way.

His parents went on disbelieving the warnings calling the event in the sky that made headlines years later a miracle. God had finally come to rescue his children.

Harold can still remember the golden light in their eyes. The way they spoke of a new beginning with the assurance of adolescence. They were taking him to be reborn when his uncle intervened saying Harold was going with him that he wasn't going to become one of those crazies like them. Liam and Harold's father fought but Liam got the upper hand and kept Harold from his parents. Harold was confused but he did whatever his uncle asked. His uncle was spirited yet determined. He was someone Harold could look up to and he protected his nephew for as long as he could. He sometimes would sing Harold to sleep with a song his grandmother used to sing to him whenever he was upset just so he wouldn't miss his parents so badly. It was about showing your true colors, that you should let them come shining through, that they are as beautiful as a rainbow. His grandmother said the song was old when she was young and had been passed down through the family because it had such tenderness of meaning and believed that everyone was special inside. He can hear the lovely tone of her tenor voice even now and the powerful emotions that were conveyed in him by the soulfulness contained in the melody and the inspired words. The song had always been the perfect antidote for his worries as it was now, so he sang it to himself. Sang it over and over until he couldn't recall anything but that song.

When his shoulder was shaken by the rough thrust of a hand he sat up abruptly, not aware that he had fallen asleep. He was stiff and his whole side ached from sleeping on the wooden floor but there looming over him and retrieving her hand from his shoulder was a girl lit by candlelight. Her alarming blue eyes and starkly contained features were as real as the fragrant breath lighting on his face. She was offering him a steaming cup of chicken noodle soup and as he blinked and tried to adjust to this new, unexpected development he realized just how hungry he was, grabbing at the soup with mumbled apologies and gobbling it down, noodles and all. Taking in its aroma and salty, brothy flavor. It tasted so wonderful that he had to force himself to slow down or else most of the soup would end up on his chin or stain his shirt.

As he observed the girl through the steam coming up out of the cup she avoided his gaze before proceeding to examine his head wound and his bandaged arm with deft fingers, retreating swiftly. She was made uncomfortable by the touch, and he found this curious.

She took the cup away before he could lap up every drop on his tongue and for a moment he was bewildered, astonished, and then he saw how she was frowning at him. There was something childish, almost comical in her frown.

What did she expect? He hadn't even considered the soup possibly drugged or poisoned, that's how hungry he was.

Where had he seen her before? She looked familiar somehow. The blue eyes, the short blond hair, the boyish features. That's it! She was on the other side of the street across from the bar that time he‑

"It's you!"

She took umbrage at the way he shouted but he hadn't meant to shout and the uneaten noodle that shot out of his mouth was a further sign of his shame.

When she got up to leave he grabbed hold of her wrist and she was startled.

"It is you, isn't it? I know you."

She had this wild look and it all centered on his grasp, on the hand that hooked her wrist. She was angry, wanting her hand freed, yet he pleaded for her to stay and talk to him.

She shook her head and ordered him to let go of her. When he did as she asked she seemed to change her mind, backing away from him instead of fleeing.

"I appreciate you taking care of me but I don't know you and I don't know why I am here."

She searched his face as if he was attempting to make a joke and he was made angry by the insolent gesture in her expression.

"I'm being serious."

There was the click of a door opening that had them both turning to look.

"Amy! Are you in here?"

Harold recognized the low, honeyed voice.

"Seth, is that you?"

"Harold? It couldn't be. My God."

There was a careful quickness in his step before Seth appeared out of the shadowy rows of books closest to them with a puzzled smile on his face. He had a long scar on his cheek and looked older but he otherwise appeared healthy. Harold was so taken, so overcome with emotion at seeing Seth in the flesh that he jumped at the chance to hug him.

"Well, that's something. Damn, Harold, I thought you were dead. This is one big surprise. It's most definitely made my day."

"I'm so glad to see you."

"The feeling is mutual. I didn't know it was you she brought here. Amy is not one to talk much and I try not to pressure her but man…this is great news."

"Didn't I tell you he was affectionate?" He said, turning to Amy.

Amy kept her usual silence but inside she was boiling. She didn't need another reminder of Harold. It was hard enough having him near. She didn't know how to act from one moment to the next and he had already showed her just how base and stupid he was. She didn't know what possessed her to help him. She knew it would be a mistake but she did it anyway. She must be losing her mind. And on top of all that she had to watch this hugging ritual. What was it that drove people to hug like that? It was so icky.

When the hugging ended there was a few slaps on the back.

"You can thank Amy here for saving your ass, Harold. She helped me too. I don't know what I would have done without her. There's no one but you and her now. Everything has gone to shit I'm afraid but I'm not going to dwell on that, not now with you here. Amy, you think you can indulge us with a little of that champagne you've been hiding?"

Amy twisted her lip at the request then rolled her eyes in mild irritation before leaving to get the champagne.

"She really is quite lovely, though not much of a talker."

"I don't know if I've seen the lovely part."

Seth laughed. He seemed to find it good to laugh.

Harold hoped John and Rosa would be with Seth. It would have made everything perfect. Yet Seth rid him of that fantasy.

"I don't know where they are, Harry, I wished I did. Now tell me what you've been up to and don't leave out the details. Details are what make life interesting."

CHAPTER 9

Over the next couple of days Harold eat what they brought him and exercised and soon he was back to his old self. Having Seth around to talk to and to joke with had made all the difference and although the lingering effects of his withdrawal had vanished the headaches were coming back with a vengeance, yet Seth had a solution.

"Amy got me those inhibitors John spoke of. They're effective just like John said they would be in getting that sun monster out of your head, but I've had memory problems on occasion so I use them sparingly. I think it is because I have an old brain. You know, memory can be a problem anyway for older people. They might work just fine for you."

"Or the memory problem is a dangerous side effect."

"I think it's worth the risk if we can get pass the borders of the city without experiencing the kind of headaches that thing can devise that make migraines appear like child's play, don't you?"

"How was she able to get the inhibitors? We haven't been-

Seth interrupted him smiling like a contented father, "Do you remember what John said about autistics, how their brains are different from normal brains. I don't know what part of the brain it is that controls emotion but theirs is underdeveloped in that area and maybe that is the key to why that thing can't get into her head. She told me they already tried to change her and it didn't work. Anyway she is able to travel unhindered. She's been outside the city."

Harold was astonished. It didn't seem possible anyone could do that. He probably would have reacted the same way if Seth told him Amy had a third eye.

"I gave her John's directions for the Edwards Research Laboratory south of here and she said it was basically a cinch getting in. There were no guards and the security alarms and cameras weren't functioning and she found the codes to the backup lock mechanisms."

"She couldn't have walked there. It has got to be what...twenty miles."

Seth shook his head. His smile growing even wider, "She is full of lots of talent, Harry. Her father was a mechanic and a master criminal on the side. He taught her how to start vehicles without a key or key fob. She talks about him as if he was a hero to her. He glows in her presence. She said he didn't treat her like any dumb girl, that he respected her. It is one of the few times she has spoken more than a sentence to me and with such enthusiasm you wouldn't know it was her speaking. Anyway, it turns out a lot of people have abandoned their vehicles with a full or half tank of gas in them. She's had her pick throughout the city. I guess religious freaks don't have much use for transportation or gas once they've been reborn. Did you notice you don't hear many planes or helicopters flying overhead?"

"I don't think I'd fly if I knew that thing was up there."

"That's a point I hadn't considered."

"But if she can drive away from here free and clear why doesn't she do that? What's keeping her here... you?"

"Nah, I don't think so. She has been roaming in and out long before we met."

"Then what is it? I know if I could be gone, I'd be gone."

"I can't say, and there's no reason to look a gift horse in the mouth. She's here to help us. We can get out of this city and I think now is the time we did that."

"You mean she's willing to help you. All this was planned before I came, wasn't it?"

"It doesn't matter. The point is you're here and now all three of us can go together."

"You sound like you wish we'd left yesterday."

"I wouldn't have thought that a week ago but events have changed. There isn't as much noise out there and the word is Jacob's armed revolution is faltering. I still have old friends in among his group who update me now and again. Morale is bad and there have been desertions. The sunbies will have control of the city soon, you can bet on that. Most everyone is dead or changed. We might not have the choice to leave if we don't do it soon."

"But there might be others we can take with us. There's John and Rosa for one. I think I should try to find them."

"I thought you'd say that. You're a good lad, Harry."

"Just give me a little time. Two days maybe."

"You have my blessing, but any more time than that would be dangerous. Amy can be ready in hours supplying us with a fully loaded vehicle. Food, water, a first aid kit, weapons which I'm not happy about but she insists on, medicine, the whole shebang. All we got to do is be there."

"Alright, I getcha', two days. I'm as ready to get out of this city as you are. Now where are those inhibitors?"

"It's getting bad, huh?"

"Bad is not the word. I never knew how easy I had it before."

"That stuff is addictive, Harry. Jacob should have never allowed for its usage. You can't just blur the edges of the intrusion you have to wipe it out entirely."

"Do they know about the inhibitors?"

Seth sighed, "I've thought about that but there isn't enough. I wish there was."

During the time Harold was recovering and Seth and he were becoming reacquainted Amy had stayed in the background keeping her covert status while eyeing Seth with respect and Harold with trepidation. Harold, though, learned to like the awkward way she spoke and the way she hid from him. There was something very curious about Amy and something loveable in the way she spurted about. She was like a firefly, lighting here and there, and her unease made him chuckle.

Harold bet that she probably liked bopping him over the head and she would probably bop him over the head again if he tried anything, yet he was intrigued.

He wondered if she knew how pretty she was, how charming her laugh was on those rare occasions when he could get her to laugh. In some odd sense he missed her when she wasn't around. She was different from any girl he has known and he knew she was attracted to him. That lack of eye contact and the blushing were clear signs. She was like a little girl unable to express her feelings.

Like Seth said she's autistic so Harold had to be careful with her.

He has never known anyone who was autistic. John told him about how the mind of autistics worked to varying degrees so her behavior toward him made sense. She was the complete opposite to Sara. Someone more in league with him.

It's weird how quickly things could change, but he wanted to know her and he meant really know her. It wasn't just her proximity or her strange idiosyncrasies that attracted him, it was something more and he need to know what that something was. It couldn't be that he was in love with her. No, he had to put that thought right out of his mind if that was the case, that was crazy, just plain crazy.

Colder Avenue had suffered from the after effects of the fighting. There was debris and devastation, broken windows, shattered pavements, rattled houses, and pools of blood and clothing everywhere. An avenue pitched into the hell of warfare. Yet among the devastation you could see a few courageous souls surveying the damage with heavy hearts. Among these courageous souls there was Adam with a rifle slung to his back looking dirty and worn and weighted down with a responsibility he probably never imagined, yet when he glimpsed Harold eyeing him from a few feet away he smiled in his old churlish way like a boy grown too old too fast.

"Good old Harry. The guy with nine lives."

"I'm using them up quickly. How about you?"

"I've had the singular honor of becoming our group's new leader."

He didn't seem too happy to say this.

"Jacob never survived the blast. I guess you have a right to know. We did everything we could. I've had to improve morale. It's not easy."

Hearing the news only confirmed what Harold feared was true.

"Now don't take what I'm saying the wrong way. I'm not blaming you."

"I never liked the guy but I think I might have judged him too quickly."

"We all have our demons."

"Yes we do, and on that note do you think you might visit your father? He misses you."

Adam's face broke out in an astonishment that quickly faded, "I knew you two would hook up somehow. You don't have to tell me how this happened. It's probably better I don't know. I don't think he wants to see me. Besides, there's too much to do."

Harold saw the ring on his left hand and felt a stab of despair rise up in him as he thought of Sara. The ring shined amid all the dirt and the scattered damage to Adam's skin.

"You two got married I see?"

Adam brought up his hand and danced his fingers with pride before Harold's face. The ring glowed in the wave of his movement and the glow had the effect of dispelling all his grief as he grinned with the undying bliss of someone in love, "She consented. It was a short ceremony but a memorable one. We took a lot of flak for wanting to be married, but whatever happens happens, right? We'll still have each other."

Like someone blindly snatched into the throes of love he was unaware of the effect he was having on Harold.

"So, there's no end to your betrayal."

Adam darted his eyes at his old friend in a tumult of confusion that turned to anger, "I didn't betray anyone, least of all you. This was for the good of all of us. I can't help it if you're too thick-headed to understand that."

"And who's this 'us' Adam? Where are they?"

Adam became furious, lifting and pointing his rifle at Harold with menace.

"And where were you?! Tell me that coward!"

Harold eyed the nozzle that was pointed at his face and didn't flinch.

"Go ahead, shoot me, if that's the only thing you know to do."

Adam sneered and lowered the rifle, pushing Harold away from him, "Go on, get out of my sight! You make me sick!"

Harold stood there for a moment before giving up. In his mind he could hear and feel the blast as if he was reliving it over and over again. It would never leave him, all those people who died trying to protect him, but he couldn't express how he felt to Adam. Adam had names for people like him and he was through listening.

As he left Colder Avenue he happened to run into an ongoing battle being waged in the main section of the city. Both the changed and unchanged were armed and fighting at full bore intensity, unafraid and assured of their cause, yet the unchanged were outnumbered and in amongst the fighting a giant golden spider roamed and pounced on the newly dead to feed and to give encouragement to its troops. Living or dead, it thrived on the energy humans could provide and while Harold saw the spider the sunbies saw a golden man praying over the dead.

The horrific sight laid waste on Harold's soul. So much had changed in two months but he should have known this was the way it was going to be, he had seen it in his grandmother's vision. Yet imagining such a possibility wasn't the same as seeing it. Seth was right, they didn't have much time.

A rifle shot cut close by. He could hear the zing of the bullet zip past him shattering a window. He leaned in to catch a sniper on the shopping plaza's roof and swiftly sped for cover as another bullet grazed the brick cornice of a building he took cover in. He'd have to get out of there real quick or he would become one of the dead being chopped to bits and tossed into the belly of that monster. There was no rest for anyone, even the dead. But getting out from his hiding place proved harder than getting in and once out he had to zigzag like mad and use the vehicles on the street for additional cover but he finally found an alley then a cross street that got him out of the mess though he was out of breath when he was finished and had to rest.

CHAPTER 10

Seth said that Liam could come with them if he wanted to and Harold felt he owed his uncle the chance to decide even if he wasn't sure the old man was capable of leaving what had become his full time sanctuary. Harold would have to convince him somehow. After all he was the only family Harold had left. Yet as he stood in front of the bar and looked up at the windows something was nagging at him. He couldn't figure out what it was but something was telling him to turn around and go, to leave before it was too late, and when he later unlocked the door to the apartment that something pressed against him yet again and if he hadn't witnessed the chaos before him he might have backed away. The apartment was in a terrible mess. The table was overturned and the camera was smashed. The mirror on the other side of the table was shattered into pieces. There were trails of blood on the carpet and dust and old torn up corpses of mice peppered about, but the most horrendous sight of all came when Harold saw the body lying on the floor in a fetal position. He gasped as he got a good look at it and wanted to cry. The whole side of his uncle's face was bloodied and the gun that had shattered his skull was still in his hand. It's no wonder he didn't want to come in. Something had indeed been trying to warn him; perhaps it had even been someone. Hadn't he felt that pressure that push as he first came in, and hadn't he also heard a voice, a voice that sounded an awful lot like his grandmother's telling him to go back. Could he be mistaken? He didn't think he was.

There was a piece of paper lying beside his uncle's shoulder. He didn't think he had the strength to lift it into his hands but he eventually found the strength.

Sorry nephew,

It's time I joined Adelia. I hope I'm sent to the right place. I should have done this long ago. I can't live this way anymore. This was the only way it couldn't get to me. My mind is mine now and if I'm cold by the time you read this then I've succeeded in fooling it. Take care and if you can find it in your heart to forgive me please do. You know I loved your mother and you and I always will.

There was no signature but Harold didn't expect there would be. His uncle hated the use of unnecessary words. Besides the love part was all that was needed. If only he had got here a little earlier.

He could hear his grandmother weeping at his back and as he heard her he felt the tears welling up in him as well. He made no effort to stem the flow that poured from him as his whole body shook from the tenderness and the sadness he felt for his uncle. He remembered how he was and maybe how he'd been at the end. A good soul all in all who had been twisted into something unrecognizable like so many of us have.

As Harold reached out to his uncle to be able to touch him one last time he could feel how cold he was. He had got his last wish. Leave it to him to find an angle that was both crazy and dignified.

Harold decided there and then that he would bury Liam next to his Aunt Adelia at Hope Cemetery come what may but he would need a vehicle first.

It took a lot of convincing by Seth to get Amy to agree to steal a Ford Ranger for the task. Seth helped Harold lift Liam into the back. They covered up his head the best way they could. He was stiff and heavy but they managed it. Amy powered up a backhoe at the cemetery and Harold dug the hole with directions from Amy. Apparently she had been trained to operate a backhoe as well. Afterwards Harold said a few words and prayed for his uncle's soul. Seth came up with an appropriate passage from the bible and they stood around in silence and respect. The wind heating at their backs as the distant sound of gunfire disturbed the silence.

Amy surprised Harold when she grabbed violets from a nearby gravesite and distributed them on his uncle's and his aunt's grave. It was a kind thing to do even if it wasn't ethical.

When she stood up from the grave her eyes caught on his as if seeking approval and when he smiled she smiled in turn. Maybe it hadn't taken all that much convincing after all.

Harold spent all of the next day in search of John and Rosa. Amy helped even though she knew Rosa had become an earth mother of sorts to the sunbies while John was heading the faction seeking peace among the group. It was a small faction but their god was playing the two-sided card most gods play in encouraging the separate ideals. A god must be merciful and ruthless if he is to maintain credibility and since the faction on the wrong side of the equation in his view was so weak he saw no need to change his stance as long as there was still a ripe supply of human energy for him to consume.

Maybe it would be the right thing to do to tell Seth and Harold the truth but she would rather spare their feelings. They had so little to believe in so why not give them this one thing.

When the whole day had gone by without success Harold had finally told Seth he was ready. They would leave once Amy found a replacement for the Ranger which had a bad fuel pump.

In the meanwhile Harold was doing all he could to gain Amy's attention, trying to extend that smile he saw on her face into something bigger. So he would purposely stand in her way and wouldn't let her pass until she made eye contact with him. She had punched him in the gut one time for doing it when he became an expert at forecasting her moves and she couldn't slip past him, but he could see that she was weakening. He could even catch a smile here or there though he dared not touch her, not just yet anyway.

Seth heard their squabbles and was delighted by them. There was nothing better than young love even in this twisted and distorted state. And though he was familiar with her anger and his acts of innocence he told Harold when he should let up. He knew Amy's limits better than Harold did. He could sense them in the tone of her voice and in her movements. The little mumbling terrors that sometimes left her frozen, almost distraught.

She had her comfort zone and it was beginning to fray but she didn't want to go back to the way things were. She found that she didn't like being alone, not entirely, that maintaining her distance had become tiresome, distressing, and a part of her wanted to try and be different from the way she was but it was the hardest thing she ever had to face, yet Seth told her not to be scared and she tried her best not to be. Seth said that Harold wouldn't do anything that she didn't want him to do, that he could talk to him if she wanted him to. Yet the mere mention of those things would cause a frenzied feeling to bubble in her gut. Still it was like exploring new territory and she has always been willing to do that. And all Harold was doing was trying to be cute, funny, even when he was asking her all these questions. It was that idea of new territory all over again. Besides, he wasn't as bad as she first thought. Maybe not the person she dreamed about but that was okay. He did have a lot of good qualities. He admired her abilities for one.

CHAPTER 11

Adam was in trouble, he just knew it. Seth could see him trapped by that thing with an army of sunbies advancing on all sides. He was plagued by the thought daily but he never let on because of the headaches that came in advance of the thought. That sun thing could be planting the thought in his head but that didn't make him any less worried about Adam. Even if his son wanted nothing to do with him he had to know he was alright. He couldn't leave without knowing and even though he was frantic he would disguise his feelings to Harold and Amy. They wouldn't allow him to see his son. They'd be concerned about his safety. And besides having Harold with him would only upset his son and he wouldn't risk Amy's life. He had to do this on his own. Somehow he knew he had to do this on his own for everything to turn out right. Adam and Sara would have to come with them. He'd convince them. He had to. The headaches would go away then and he would be able to sleep. Nothing was going to stop him.

CHAPTER 12

Harold wasn't crazy about the choice Amy made given the truck's color. To him the Toyota Tundra stood out like a beacon and would create undue attention but Amy pushed aside his criticism saying the truck would light up like a fire ball burning through the streets, cleansing everything it came in contact with, so what was so wrong with that.

"I thought you were the type that didn't like attention."

The matter was closed, red it was and red it was going to stay. Harold shook his head, admiring her spirit.

"I'll help you load up if you want."

Amy said she could handle it. She would rather have him keep an eye on Seth, his memory lapses were getting worse. Harold didn't think the lapses were all that bad believing Seth simply needed time to rest. He was just stressed, that's all, they all were stressed. The sooner they left the city the better.

"Just do it, okay?"

"Whatever you say, ma'am."

Harold watched her work in open-mouthed wonder as she circumvented the computer and started the engine. Was there anything she couldn't do? She was sweating by the time she finished. That was the first time he saw her sweat, he kind of liked it.

When they returned with the truck Seth wasn't where they left him in the storage area of the library. He said he was going to fill the time while they were gone with assessing their inventory but he wasn't in the storage area, though this didn't seem to be a big deal since they knew he had a tendency to get bored, needing a new stimulant to spark his interest, they went exploring. It was near the end of the day so they guessed he had probably gone up to the language section to continue brushing up on the Mandarin he was learning through one of the instruction books in braille. But he wasn't in the language section or anywhere else. Usually he saw every part of the library as his own little home away from home and Harold hadn't taken his wandering all that seriously even if Amy had.

And now he wanted to kick himself for being so casual about Seth's absences.

They searched outside the building and along the street, hoping he might have stepped out or lost his bearings, but Seth has never just stepped out without notifying them or lost his bearings and the search proved futile.

"He has ever done something like this?"

Amy was too occupied with bad thoughts to answer Harold's question and Harold didn't really want to know in any case. The Seth he knew would be incapable of simply disappearing, but he has had moments when he has been testy and irritable, even acting like he didn't know who Harold was, and those moments had become more frequent lately. Harold had thought that his sleeplessness was responsible but what if something else was bothering him.

That was just the thing. At one moment he would be enjoying Harold and Amy's company and at the next his face would twist strangely and he would be irritable, saying he was suffocating and needed to be alone.

Amy had to remind him to take his inhibitors. The testiness and the irritability were resulting from the headaches, and short of her feeding him his pills directly which he would have taken as an insult she had to live with his assurances that he was keeping up with the dosages.

"C'mon, let's get in the truck and search the neighborhood. He couldn't have gone far."

A few minutes after they started out Seth was spotted turning down Delaware. They were immediately relieved to see him even in his current dogged condition. He was shambling along on tired feet looking distraught as he called out to his son. Seth didn't respond to them as they pulled up beside him. He returned to shouting as Amy parked the truck and they got out.

"Stop it, Seth! What are you doing?"

Seth held back from his hollering to turn to Harold. His face had changed slightly beneath the shades. He seemed to be disoriented, straining to concentrate, "Is that you, Harold?"

"Yea, it is, now get in the truck."

Amy was struck by a feeling that they were being watched. She looked about and saw sunbies appearing on the roofs, on the streets, some of them were armed. She grabbed onto Harold's arm and pointed them out to him.

"Okay, Seth, now we've really got to go."

"But my son. He's here somewhere, I know it."

A shot rang out from the rooftops and Seth was hit in the chest. Harold and Amy quickly grabbed hold of him and threw him into the truck, not bothering to look and see where the shot came from. There were more. The truck was besieged with bullets. The driver's side window was shattered, the windshield was cracked, and a headlight blown out as Amy sped away from the curb. The left front tire was hit seconds later and then a rear tire. They had to abandon the truck. They carried Seth into a shopping center under gunfire and hid behind the jewelry counter as the shooting continued checking Seth's condition. The bullet missed his heart but hit a lung. He was bleeding from the mouth and struggling to breathe. Of all the talents Amy had she didn't know how to remove a bullet and neither did Harold.

"I know of a doctor who could help him but we need a vehicle." Amy said.

"We can't go out in that."

"I know, but she isn't in the city and we don't have the time."

There was more shooting. A larger barrage, a battle. Sunbies were flooding into the store with Rosa at the head. Her golden eyes had zeroed in on Harold and Amy with uncommon efficiency as if instructed to do so.

"I can help. You know I was a nurse, Harold. Let me help."

Harold was shocked. It seemed like all his friends were lost to him. Amy had to get him to focus, to not look at Rosa, to not be swept into her spell, its spell.

"Let me help. Let us bring him to our lord for healing."

There was a hallelujah expelled from the followers at her side yet before they could make an advance a commotion from outside made them turn and go. Rosa promised they would be coming back so they knew they couldn't stay there. Luckily Harold found a wheelbarrow in the gardening area as they made their way to the back of the shop and into a corridor ranked with other shops toward the loading area at the rear of the center. All of this took time and Seth was finding it harder and harder to breathe. They kept him on his side in order to clear his air passages but he still had problems breathing. They were afraid they were going to lose him but no other ideas came to them. They tried getting him to talk, to stop from fainting.

Harold broke a lock to pull up on the overhead door. There was a service van parked in the loading area, possibly illegally but who cared, there was no one around. There would be no greater opportunity. They worked quickly with Harold carting and distributing Seth into the van while Amy busied herself with the ignition system.

It was getting dark even though they were in the middle of the day. After Harold removed Seth from the wheelbarrow and laid him out on a canvas at the back of the van he looked up to see what was making things dark. He thought it might be a wave of clouds creating a storm but it hasn't rained in ages. What he saw instead seemed even less possible and it left him speechless. The sun was being eclipsed. He wouldn't have believed it if he hadn't seen it happening right there before his eyes. He thought he had to be dreaming.

"Amy, look, do you see?!"

"Shhh, someone will hear you."

By the time he got to the front of the van he found her waiting for him with an expression of absolute amazement and a ring of keys jingling in her hand.

"They were wedged in beside the seat."

"Damn."

The van was opened in the back so Harold could keep Seth company while still talking to Amy as she drove. They had to take the long way back to the library, curving around the sounds of battle.

Amy told Harold to stay in the truck as she went into the library. Seth's breathing was becoming shallow. He told Seth to hang on but he was becoming anxious. Seth wouldn't survive much longer and Amy seemed to be taking too long. She could be in trouble. What if there was someone inside waiting for her? He wasn't sure if there was any place that was safe and it was getting darker by the moment outside. At the same time it was getting darker, he could feel a weight being lifted from his mind. The inhibitors worked but there was still the weight of something there yet now that something had lifted off of him. He could hear the distant sound of howling, of people in the midst of bewilderment and pain. The air of battle had turned silent.

He saw Amy's pale face shoot through the gloom. She was carrying a back pack and a satchel as he flew open the doors in the back for her, grabbing on to the pack and the satchel as she handed them to him. He closed the doors as she got inside. She was out of breath but fine otherwise.

"I was afraid. I was almost going to go inside to look for you."

"I'm okay. We have at least an hour's drive ahead of us. Do you think he'll make it?"

Harold looked down at Seth. What could he say? It was anybody's guess.

"I don't know."

"Well, there's a first-aid kit in the satchel if you think of anything that could help."

The howling had gotten worse.

"What in the hell is that?"

"Just drive, okay."

There were graffiti on the side of the library. Detailed in red ink it read.

FUCK THE SUNBIES

SINNERS REPENT

BLESS OUR GOLDEN CREATOR

HOLY WAR

After they pulled out of the parking lot, they encountered a mob a couple of blocks away. Amy, without missing a beat, locked the passenger door just as someone tried to get in. All those sets of radiated golden eyes were coming out of the gloom and merging toward them. Rocks were thrown at the van. The passenger side window was busted in. A hand reached into the lock. Seth grabbed hold of a crow bar near the wheel wedge and stabbed at the hand sharply until he heard a scream and the hand recoiled. The butts of rifles were slammed against the metal sides of the van. The mob howled, they roared that God would not forsake thee. The sound was chilling, ear-splitting, but Amy kept her eyes on the road and pressed the accelerator to the floor running over bodies along the way. More objects flew within her sight and she had to duck when one of them came in close contact with her, poking a hole through the windshield instead and tumbling off the dashboard. It was a rock, some kind of rock, or maybe a piece of concrete from one of the cracked structures.

She kept driving and the howling, the clashes against the van continued. The sky had turned into a dark hole now, a dark abyss that shrank the sun's light out of existence. One headlight blared into the night showcasing the devastation as Amy touched a knob on the steering column. The other headlight hung in shatters.

The road ahead of them stretched out to the city's limit. They had to make it. They had to keep going while all around them there was madness and the darkened, cooling sky.

·The End·

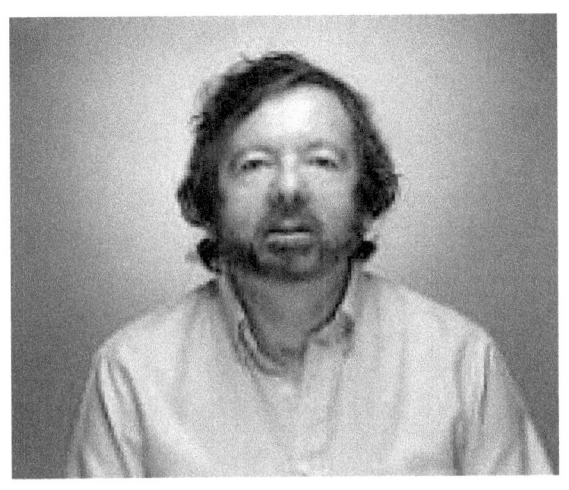

Stephen O'Rourke is a graduate of Scripps-Howard School of Journalism and the Hollywood Script-Writing Institute. He has done everything from being a farmhand to selling solar panels. His work has appeared in magazines and he lives in upstate New York.

COMING SOON

Severed Empire: Wizard's War by Phillip Tomasso

Halfway To Anywhere – A Sci/Fi short story
collection

Find these and other books at

www.mirrormatterpress.com